Pearl the Cloud Fairy

For Jean, with love and thanks for
the many pearls of wisdom!

Special thanks to
Narinder Dhami

No part of this work may be reproduced, stored in a retrieval system, or transmitted in any form or by any means, electronic, mechanical, photocopying, recording, or otherwise, without written permission of the publisher. For information regarding permission, write to Rainbow Magic Limited, c/o HIT Entertainment, 830 South Greenville Avenue, Allen, TX 75002.

ISBN-13: 978-0-439-81388-4
ISBN-10: 0-439-81388-3

12 11 10   12 13 14 15/0

Printed in the U.S.A.   40

Pearl the Cloud Fairy

by Daisy Meadows

SCHOLASTIC INC.

New York   Toronto   London   Auckland   Sydney
Mexico City   New Delhi   Hong Kong   Buenos Aires

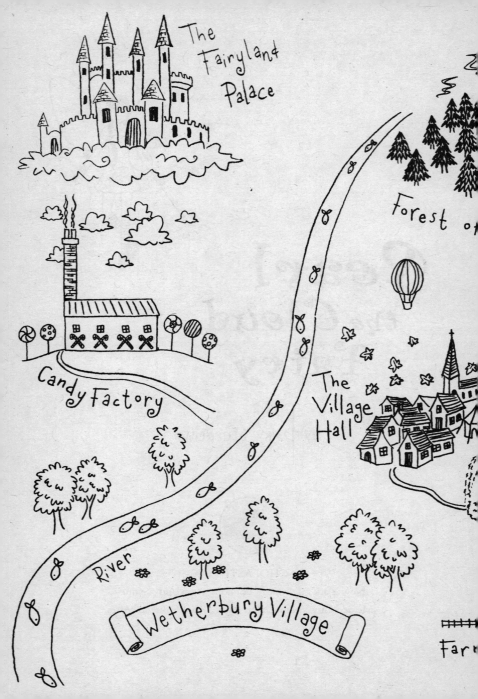

Jack Frost's Ice Castle

reen Wood

Mrs. Fordham's House

The Park

Willow Hill

High St.

The Museum

irsty's House

Fields

Mudhole

N
W — E
S

Goblins green and goblins small,
I cast this spell to make you tall.
As high as the palace you shall grow.
My icy magic makes it so.

Then steal the rooster's magic feathers,
used by the fairies to make all weathers.
Climate chaos I have planned
on Earth, and here, in Fairyland!

Contents

Missing Fidget

"What's the weather like today, Kirsty?" asked Rachel Walker eagerly. She pushed back her bedspread. "Do you think there's magic in the air?"

Kirsty Tate was standing at the bedroom window, staring out over the garden. "It seems like a normal day."

She sighed, with a disappointed look on her face. "The sky's gray and cloudy."

"Never mind." Rachel jumped out of bed and went to join her friend. "Remember what Titania, the Fairy Queen, told us. Don't look too hard for magic —"

"Because the magic will find you!" Kirsty finished with a smile.

Rachel and Kirsty shared a very special
secret. They were friends with fairies!
When Jack Frost had put a spell on the
seven Rainbow Fairies and banished
them to Rainspell Island, Rachel and
Kirsty helped them return to Fairyland.
Now Jack Frost was up to no good
again — this time with the Weather
Fairies. And once again, the Fairy King
and Queen had asked
Rachel and Kirsty for help.

"Look at Doodle."
Rachel pointed at the
weather-vane rooster,
which sat on top of the old
barn. "Don't you think he
looks a little happier, now that he has
two of his tail feathers back?"

Kirsty nodded. "Let's hope we find all

of his feathers before you go home," she replied. "Then the weather in Fairyland can get back to normal again!"

Doodle the rooster had a very important job. With his seven magic tail feathers and the help of the Weather Fairies, Doodle controlled Fairyland's weather. But then Jack Frost sent his mean goblin servants to steal Doodle's feathers. Doodle chased the goblins into the human world — but without his magic, and away from Fairyland, he changed into an ordinary, rusty weather vane!

Kirsty's dad had found the weather vane lying in the park, and brought it home to put on the roof of the barn. He had no idea what a magical creature Doodle really was!

Now the weather in Fairyland was a big mess — and it would be a mess until Rachel and Kirsty got all of Doodle's feathers back and sent him home.

"Well, we're off to a good start," said Rachel. "With the help of Crystal the Snow Fairy and Abigail the Breeze Fairy, we've already found two feathers!"

The King and Queen had promised Kirsty and Rachel that each of the Weather Fairies would come to help them find the feathers.

"Girls, are you awake?" Kirsty's mom called from downstairs. "Breakfast's ready."

"Coming!" Kirsty shouted back.

"I wish we knew what Doodle was trying to tell us yesterday," said Rachel, as she and Kirsty ran downstairs. Each time one of Doodle's tail feathers had been replaced, the rooster had come to life. The

first time, he squawked "Beware!" The second time, he managed to say the word "Jack," before turning to metal again.

"I'm sure it was something about Jack Frost," Kirsty said thoughtfully. "But what?"

"Maybe he'll tell us if we find another feather!" Rachel suggested. The girls went into the kitchen. Mr. Tate was setting the table, and Kirsty's mom was making toast.

"Morning, you two," said Mr. Tate with a smile, as the girls sat down. "What are you planning to do today?"

Before Kirsty or Rachel could answer him, there was a knock at the back door.

"I wonder who that could be!" Mrs. Tate said, raising her eyebrows. "It's still pretty early."

"I'll get it," said Kirsty, who was closest.

She opened the door. There were Mr. and Mrs. Twitching, the Tates' neighbors.

"Oh, Kirsty, good morning," said Mr.
Twitching. "We're sorry to bother you,
but we were hoping you might have seen
Fidget?"

Kirsty frowned, trying to remember.
She knew Fidget, the Twitchings' fluffy
tabby cat, very well, but she hadn't
seen her for the last day or two. "I
haven't seen her lately,"
she replied.

"Oh, dear,"
Mrs. Twitching
said, looking
upset. "She
didn't come
home for her
dinner last night."

"Come in and ask
Mom and Dad," Kirsty suggested,

opening the door wider. "Maybe they've seen her."

As Mr. and Mrs. Twitching walked into the kitchen, Kirsty blinked. For a minute, she thought she'd seen strange wisps of pale smoke curling and drifting over the neighbors' heads.

She glanced at Rachel and her parents, but they didn't seem to have noticed anything unusual. Kirsty shook her head. Maybe she was just imagining it. . . .

Magic in the Air

"When was the last time you saw Fidget?" asked Kirsty's mom as she poured some coffee for the Twitchings.

"Yesterday afternoon," Mrs. Twitching replied. "It's very strange, because usually she doesn't miss a single meal."

"Kirsty and I could help you look for her," suggested Rachel.

"Good idea," Kirsty agreed, finishing her cereal. "Let's go now."

"And I'll check our garden and the barn," added Mr. Tate.

As Kirsty and Rachel got up from the table, Kirsty stared extra-hard at the Twitchings' heads. She thought she could see wisps of smoke there again, but they were so pale and misty, it was hard to be sure.

"Rachel," Kirsty said quietly as they

headed outside, "did you notice anything funny about the Twitchings today?"

Rachel looked confused. "What do you mean?"

Kirsty told her about the wisps of smoke. "I'm not sure if I really saw them or not," she finished.

"Do you think they could have been magic?" Rachel asked.

Kirsty felt a thrill of excitement. "Maybe," she said eagerly. "While we're looking for Fidget, we'd better keep our eyes open for magic, too!"

The girls walked into the village, keeping their eyes peeled for the tabby cat, but there was no sign of her.

"I hope Fidget isn't lost for good," Kirsty said, looking around. "Oh!"

Kirsty hadn't been watching where she was going, and she'd bumped into someone. "I'm so sorry," Kirsty said politely.

The woman glared at her. "Why don't you be more careful?" she said grumpily, and hurried off.

"Well!" Rachel gasped. "That wasn't very nice."

But Kirsty looked confused. "That was Mrs. Hill, one of my mom's friends, and she's usually *very* nice," she said. "I wonder what's wrong?"

Rachel nudged her. "Look over there," she whispered.

Outside the post office, two men were arguing. They both looked very grouchy. Then Mrs. Burke, who ran the post office, came out to see what was going on. Kirsty was surprised to see that her usually happy face was grumpy and sad.

"There's something strange happening," she whispered to Rachel as they went into the park. "Everybody's in a terrible mood. Look at the kids on the swings."

Rachel stared at the children in the playground. They didn't seem to be having fun at all. Every single one of them looked sad! They didn't even cheer up when the ice-cream truck stopped close by.

The girls stopped at the park gate.

"I think we've been all over

Wetherbury, and there's no sign of Fidget anywhere." Kirsty sighed, glancing at her watch. "We'd better go home, Rachel. It's almost time for lunch."

Rachel nodded. "We can always keep searching later this afternoon."

The girls turned back toward the Tates' house. On the way, they passed the tiny movie theater. The Saturday morning show had just finished, and the audience was pouring out. Just like everyone else, the people looked grouchy.

"It must have been a sad movie," Rachel whispered to Kirsty.

"But it wasn't," Kirsty replied, frowning. "Look." She pointed to the poster outside the movie theater.

"This hilarious film is a must. You'll split  *your sides laughing,"* Rachel read. "Well, the audience definitely didn't find it very funny," she continued. "Look at their faces."

Kirsty stared at the people walking gloomily out of the theater. Suddenly, her heart began to pound. There they were again! She could definitely see cloudy smoke drifting over people's heads, just like she'd noticed over her next-door neighbors. "Look, Rachel!" She nudged her friend. "There's that smoke again."

Rachel squinted at the people who were all frowning. For a minute, she thought Kirsty was seeing things. But then she spotted them, too — thin, wispy trails of smoke, hovering over the heads of the people like little clouds.

"It must be fairy magic!" Rachel said excitedly. "I'll bet those aren't wisps of smoke at all. They're magic clouds!"

"Maybe," Kirsty agreed, her eyes lighting up. "We could be close to finding another magic feather!"

The girls rushed home. When they entered the house, the first

thing they noticed were the clouds hovering over Mr. and Mrs. Tate!

"Did you find Fidget?" asked Kirsty's mom. She was sitting on the couch, reading a book. The little white cloud over her head was tinted with pink, like a cloud in a sunset.

"No," Kirsty replied, staring at the gray cloud over her dad.

"Oh, dear," Mr. Tate said, looking sad.

"I think the goblin with the magic Cloud Feather must be close by," Rachel whispered to Kirsty as they ate their sandwiches.

Kirsty nodded. "After lunch, let's go up to my bedroom and plan our next move," she said. "These clouds are beginning to worry me."

"Me, too," Rachel agreed.

As soon as they'd finished their food, the girls ran upstairs. Kirsty threw open her bedroom door.

"Hello!" called a tiny voice. "I thought you would never come!"

There, sitting on the windowsill and swinging her legs below her, was Pearl the Cloud Fairy.

Goblin Hunting

Pearl was resting her chin on her hands, and she also looked gloomy. She wore a beautiful pink and white dress with a full skirt, and in her hand, she held a pretty pink wand. The wand had a fluffy white tip. Little pink and white sunset clouds drifted and swirled out of it.

To Kirsty's amazement, a tiny gray cloud hovered over Pearl's head. "Oh, Pearl! You have a rain cloud, too!" Kirsty said.

"I know." Pearl sighed, then her eyes flashed with annoyance. "It's because one of those nasty goblins is using the magic Cloud Feather — and he's doing it all wrong!" she snapped.

"We think the goblin must be very close, because everyone in Wetherbury

seems to have a cloud over them,"
Rachel told Pearl.

"I'm sure you're right," Pearl said.
"This is definitely fairy magic, so
that mean old goblin can't be far
away!" She fluttered up into the
air, leaving a trail of shining
pink and white clouds
behind her. "Even you
two are beginning to
get clouds now!"
she added.

The girls rushed
over to the mirror
to look. Sure
enough, tiny gray
clouds were starting to
form over their heads.

"Should we go find the Cloud Feather?" Kirsty asked eagerly.

Pearl and Rachel both cheered up at that suggestion. Pearl zoomed over to hide herself in Rachel's jacket pocket. Then they all headed out into the village.

This time, Rachel and Kirsty could see the clouds over people's heads much more clearly. Some were a pretty pink or orange color, and the people underneath them seemed quiet and dreamy.

Other clouds were black and stormy, and the people under those looked gloomy and annoyed. Some clouds were drizzling tiny raindrops, making their people look very sad. And a few very angry people had clouds with little lightning bolts over their heads.

"Look." Rachel nudged Kirsty as a man with a lightning cloud hurried past, scowling.

"His hair's standing straight up like he got an electric shock!"

"Pearl," Kirsty whispered. "Why hasn't anyone else noticed the clouds?"

Pearl popped her head out of Rachel's pocket. "Only magic beings like fairies  can see them," she replied. "And you two, because you're helping us."

"The clouds are getting bigger," said Rachel, staring at a woman who passed by with an enormous rain cloud over her head.

"We must be getting closer to the feather!" Pearl said eagerly.

"But where can it be?" Kirsty wondered. "We're almost out of the village now." She stopped and looked around. Suddenly, she gasped, and pointed at a building to their left. "Look at the candy factory!"

The candy factory stood right on the edge of Wetherbury. A stream of small pink and white clouds were puffing out of the tall brick chimney.

"The goblin must be hiding inside the factory," Pearl cried, whizzing out of Rachel's pocket and fluttering up into the air. "It's time to rescue the Cloud Feather!"

A Sticky Situation

"Come on," Rachel said. "Let's go inside."

The girls and Pearl rushed over to the door. But their hearts sank when they saw the big, heavy padlock.

"Of course, it's Saturday. The factory's closed." Kirsty said, looking disappointed. "What are we going to do?"

They stood and thought for a minute. Then Rachel glanced up, and a smile spread across her face. "Look!" she said, pointing. "There's an air vent near the roof. We have our magic fairy dust. Let's turn ourselves into fairies. Then we can all fly in through the air vent."

The Fairy Queen had given Kirsty and Rachel gold lockets full of fairy dust, which they could use to turn themselves into fairies whenever they needed to.

"Good idea!" Pearl laughed, clapping her hands happily.

Quickly, Rachel and
Kirsty opened their
lockets and sprinkled
some fairy dust over
themselves. Almost
immediately, they
began to shrink, and
beautiful shimmering
fairy wings grew from
their backs.

"Come on," Pearl cried, zooming
back and forth impatiently. "Up we go!"
And she flew up to the air vent in the
wall.

Kirsty and Rachel flew after her. Pearl
slipped through the vent first, and the
two girls followed. They all stopped
inside and gazed around the factory.

"Wow!" Kirsty gasped, her eyes wide.

Lots of big silver machines were busy
making all kinds of different candy.
Peppermints poured out of one machine,
while long strings of strawberry licorice
came out of another. Soft ice cream
fizzed into paper cups, and pink and
white marshmallows bounced along a
moving conveyor belt. Chocolate bars

were being wrapped in gold foil, while a
different machine wrapped caramel
candies in shiny silver paper. There were
large sticky lollipops and striped candy
canes in every color and flavor.

"Isn't this amazing?" asked Rachel.
"Look at all the different kinds of
candy!"

Kirsty looked confused. "But the people who work here wouldn't have left all the machines on, would they?" she pointed out.

Pearl grinned. "I bet they turned them off, but somebody else has turned them on again."

"The goblin!" Kirsty exclaimed. "Where is he?"

"Let's split up and see if we can find him," Pearl replied.

They flew off to different parts of the factory. Rachel flew toward a machine that was mixing fluffy pink cotton candy in a huge silver tub.

She looked at the machine for a minute
and was about to fly on, but then she
heard the sound of someone loudly
smacking his lips.

Rachel flew down
to take a closer
look. There,
lying with his
back to her, on a
huge, fluffy pink
cloud, was the
goblin! He was
greedily scooping
up sticky handfuls
of cotton candy and
munching them happily. He
was quite chubby — probably from
stuffing himself with so much cotton
candy, Rachel thought.

She flew a little closer and peeked over the goblin's shoulder to see if she could spot the magic Cloud Feather. There it was, in his hand! Tiny pink and white clouds drifted from it as the goblin waved it in the air.

I have to tell Kirsty and Pearl, Rachel thought. She turned to fly away, but as she did, one wing brushed the goblin's shoulder. With a yelp of surprise, the goblin reached up and grabbed Rachel with one hand.

"You're not getting my feather!" he shouted, and stuffed Rachel inside one of the pink clouds that was drifting by.

Poor Rachel was trapped! She tried to push her way out of the cloud, but she couldn't make a hole in it. The cloud drifted farther and farther away from the goblin.

"Kirsty! Pearl!" Rachel called as loudly as she could. "HELP!"

Kirsty heard her friend's voice right away. She turned and saw the cloud with Rachel inside. It was floating past the marshmallow machine.

To Kirsty's horror, the cloud was heading straight toward the factory's tall chimney.

"Oh no!" Kirsty gasped. "If that cloud floats up the chimney, we'll never get Rachel back!"

Cotton Candy Clouds

Quickly, Pearl flew over to Kirsty.
"Which cloud is Rachel in?" she asked.

"That one . . ." Kirsty began, pointing.
Then she stopped. There were so many
clouds floating around, she'd lost sight of
Rachel. "Oh, I don't know anymore,
Pearl. That awful goblin did it!" she said.

"I have a few things to say to him! Can you make me human-size again?"

Pearl nodded. "Don't worry," she said, "I'll find Rachel. I promise. You get the feather back."

With a wave of her wand, Pearl turned Kirsty back to her normal size. Then she flew off to search through the clouds. Kirsty stormed over to the goblin. She was usually scared of the nasty creatures — especially since Jack Frost had used his magic to make them even bigger than before. But Kirsty was so annoyed, she didn't care. Rachel was in danger, and it was all the goblin's fault.

The goblin was lying on top of his fluffy cloud, still eating cotton candy. When he saw Kirsty marching toward him, he looked nervous. Quickly, he stuffed the Cloud Feather right into his mouth.

"Give me that feather!" Kirsty demanded.

"Wha' fe'er?" the goblin spluttered, trying to keep his mouth closed.

Kirsty frowned. How was she going to get the feather out of the goblin's mouth? Just then, she spotted a peppermint stick lying on the floor. That gave her an idea. She picked it up, and began tickling the bottom of the goblin's leathery foot!

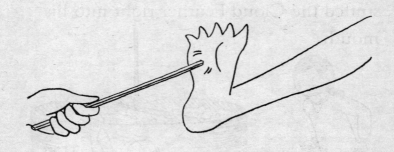

The goblin began to laugh, but he kept his mouth shut. "Shtop it," he mumbled. But then he couldn't hold his laughter in anymore. "Oh, ha ha ha," he laughed. As his laughter burst out, so did the magic Cloud Feather!

Kirsty tried to grab the feather, but the

goblin was quicker.

"Oh no!" He grinned, snatching the feather away. "This is *my* feather! I'm the only one who knows how to make it work."

"Actually, I know how to make it work, too!" called a silvery voice.

Kirsty turned to see Pearl flying toward them. To Kirsty's relief, she was pulling a pink cloud behind her with Rachel inside.

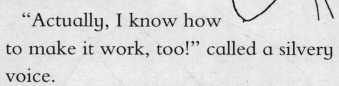

Rachel's head was sticking out of a hole in the cloud, and she grinned at Kirsty. "Hey, this cloud's made of cotton candy!" she called. "And it's delicious. I can eat my way out!" She took another big bite of the cloud.

Pearl flew down to Kirsty and the goblin. "I can make the clouds do all sorts of things," she said. "They will float exactly where I tell them to. I can even make them dance around me." She held out her hand to the goblin. "Why don't you give me the feather and let me show you?"

The goblin looked sly. "No, it's mine!" he said. "Anyway, I can do those tricks myself."

"Go on, then," Pearl challenged.

The goblin began to concentrate. He waved the feather around in the air. Very slowly, all the clouds in the room drifted toward him. He twirled the feather, and the clouds began to spin around him in a circle, faster and faster. "See?" the goblin bragged.

"OK, you know what to do, Rachel," Pearl whispered to her.

Pearl let go of Rachel's cotton candy cloud, and she and Kirsty watched as it flew over to the goblin. Rachel's cloud began to whirl around him with the others. It got closer and closer to the goblin. Then, suddenly, as her cloud sped past the goblin's hand, Rachel stuck her arm out and grabbed the Cloud Feather!

A Silver Lining

"Give that back!" the goblin shouted.
Every time Rachel's cloud flew past him,
he tried to grab back the feather, but he
missed over and over again.

The clouds were spinning around so
fast now that Rachel was getting very
dizzy. "Help!" she called. "Somebody
stop this cloud!"

Pearl swooped down and plucked
the feather out of Rachel's
hand. Then she waved it
in a special pattern, and
the clouds began to
slow down and
drift away.

Kirsty caught
Rachel's cloud with
one hand, and she
pulled it open to
free her friend.

Rachel dizzily
tumbled out. The
goblin was dizzy,
too, from watching
all the clouds
spinning around
his head.

He was walking in circles, looking for the Cloud Feather. When he saw that Pearl had it, he lunged forward and grabbed for her. Pearl flew out of the way just in time, but the goblin lost his balance. He tripped and fell headfirst into the candy wrapping machine!

The girls and Pearl watched in amazement as the yelling goblin was wrapped in a huge sheet of shiny silver paper. Then the goblin-shaped candy moved along the conveyor belt, and was wrapped with a sparkly silver ribbon.

"That serves him right!" Rachel laughed.

"Come on," said Pearl, smiling. "Let's get out of here before he unwraps himself!"

Kirsty sprinkled herself with fairy dust and immediately turned into a fairy again. Then the three friends flew out of the factory through the air vent. Outside, Pearl waved her magic wand and returned the girls to their normal size.

"I'd better make sure everyone else in Wetherbury gets back to normal right away!" Pearl laughed.

She waved her feather through the air in a complicated pattern. "That should do it," she said cheerfully. They set off for the Tates' house, and Pearl hid in Rachel's pocket again.

"Look," whispered Rachel, as they made their way through the village. "There aren't any clouds over people's heads anymore!"

"And everyone's happy and laughing again," added Kirsty. The kids playing in the park were all smiling now, and as the girls passed the post office, Mrs. Burke gave them a cheerful wave.

"I'll give Doodle his beautiful Cloud Feather back," Pearl said, when they arrived at the Tates' house. "He'll be so happy to see it!"

Rachel and Kirsty stood in the garden. They watched as Pearl flew up to the top of the barn. The fairy placed the Cloud Feather in Doodle's tail. A minute later, the rooster's feathers began to sparkle with fairy magic.

"Doodle's coming to life again!" Kirsty cried. "Listen up, Rachel!"

Doodle's feathers shimmered in the sun. "Frost w —!" he squawked. But the next minute, he was cold, hard metal again.

"Beware, Jack Frost w —" Kirsty said thoughtfully, as Pearl flew down to join them. "What does it mean?"

"I don't know," replied Pearl. "But be careful. Jack Frost won't want to lose any more magic feathers! And now I have to return to Fairyland."

The pretty fairy hugged Rachel and Kirsty, scattering little, shiny pink and white clouds around them. Then she fluttered up into the sky. "Good-bye!" she called, "And thank you! Good luck finding the other four weather feathers!"

"Good-bye!" called Kirsty and Rachel, waving.

Smiling, Pearl waved her wand at them and disappeared into the clouds.

The girls went into the house, where Mr. and Mrs. Tate were in the living room watching TV.

"Oh, Kirsty, Rachel, there you are," said Mrs. Tate, jumping to her feet. "The Twitchings called a little while ago and invited us over for coffee."

"And they said they have some good news for us," Mr. Tate added.

Kirsty and Rachel looked at each other.

"They must have found Fidget!" Kirsty exclaimed happily.

The girls hurried next door with Mr. and Mrs. Tate.

Mr. Twitching opened the door with a big smile on his face. "Come in," he said. "We've got a surprise for you!"

He led them into the living room, where Mrs. Twitching 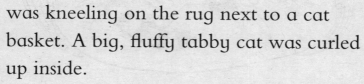 was kneeling on the rug next to a cat basket. A big, fluffy tabby cat was curled up inside.

"She's been a very busy girl," Mrs. Twitching said proudly. "Look!"

There in the basket were three tiny kittens, snuggled up close to their mom.

Two were tabby cats like Fidget, and
one was black with a little white spot on
the top of its head. They were so young,
their eyes weren't even open yet.

"Oh, Rachel, aren't they beautiful?"
Kirsty whispered, gently stroking the
black and white kitten on its tiny head.

"We'll be looking for good homes for
them when they're bigger," said Mr.
Twitching. "But they can't leave their
mom for eight or nine weeks."

"Oh!" Kirsty gasped, her eyes shining. "Maybe I could have one?"

"I don't see why not," Mrs. Tate said, smiling.

"Which one would you like, Kirsty?" Mrs. Twitching asked.

"This one," Kirsty said, stroking the black and white kitten again. It yawned sleepily.

"And I know the perfect name for her," Rachel said, smiling at her friend. "You can call her Pearl!"

RAINBOW magic™

THE WEATHER FAIRIES

Pearl's weather feather has been
returned, but now Rachel and Kirsty
must help

Goldie
the Sunshine Fairy!

Join their next adventure
in this special sneak peek!

A Sunny Spell

"I feel like I'm going to melt," said
Rachel Walker happily.

It was a hot summer afternoon and she
and her friend, Kirsty Tate, were enjoying
the sunshine in Kirsty's backyard.

The weather was so warm and sunny
that Mr. and Mrs. Tate had given the
girls permission to camp out in the yard
that night.

Kirsty put two sleeping bags inside the tent and then flopped down on the grass. "Phew!" she said, and whistled. "It's still so hot! I hope it cools down soon, or we'll never be able to sleep in there." Rachel was frowning and looking at her watch.

"Kirsty," she said slowly. "Have you noticed where the sun is?"

Kirsty looked up and pointed. "Right there, in the sky," she replied.

"Yes, but look how high it is," Rachel insisted. "It hasn't even *started* setting yet."

Kirsty glanced at her watch. "But it's seven-thirty," she said, frowning. "That can't be right."